Also by Jeanne Willis and Tony Ross:

*Cottonwool Colin*

*Grill Pan Eddy*

*Mammoth Pie*

*Old Dog*

First American edition published in 2009 by Andersen Press USA,
an imprint of Andersen Press Ltd. www.andersenpressusa.com

Text copyright © 2009 by Jeanne Willis
Illustrations © 2009 by Tony Ross

Distributed in the United States and Canada by
Lerner Publishing Group, Inc.
241 First Avenue North
Minneapolis, MN 55401 U.S.A.
www.lernerbooks.com

Library of Congress Cataloging-in-Publication Data Available
ISBN: 978−0−7613−5151−1

Manufactured in Singapore.
1 2 3 4 5 6        14 13 12 11 10 09

# FLABBY CAT
### AND
# SLOBBY DOG

JEANNE WILLIS

TONY ROSS

ANDERSEN PRESS USA

Flabby Cat was sitting on the sofa when in came Slobby Dog.
He sat next to her like he'd always done since they were small.
But today, they just couldn't get comfortable.
"I'm all squashed," said Slobby Dog. "This sofa has shrunk."
"Nonsense!" said Flabby Cat. "The cushions have grown."
"That's it," said Slobby Dog.
"It's very uncomfortable. Whatever shall we do?" said Flabby Cat.
"Let's do what we always do," said Slobby Dog.

So they ate and ate and ate.

And they slept and slept and slept.

It was all very comforting, but when they woke up . . .

. . . the sofa had shrunk even smaller.

And the cushions had grown even **bigger**. Or so they liked to think.

"It's a frightful squeeze," said Slobby Dog.
"Whatever shall we do now?" asked Flabby Cat.
"What we always do," said Slobby Dog.

So they ate and **ate** and **ate**.

And they slept and **slept** and **slept**.

It was all very comforting, but when they woke up . . .

. . . the sofa had practically disappeared.
And the cushions almost filled the room. Or so they imagined.

"We'll never get comfortable!" sighed Slobby Dog.
"Whatever shall we do?" cried Flabby Cat. "Eat and sleep?"

. . . watch TV!"

So that's what they did.

They watched a show
about a cunning tiger
and a wild wolf. And while
they were watching . . .

. . . they ate and ate and ate.

And they slept and slept and slept.

It was all very comforting, but when they woke up . . .

"There's no room for us here," said Flabby Cat. "Wherever shall we live?"

"Perhaps the cunning tiger and the wild wolf will let us live with them," said Slobby Dog.

"They are our distant relatives, after all," agreed Flabby Cat. "Let's go and ask."

But their distant relatives were a lot more distant than they thought. Slobby Dog and Flabby Cat walked and walked through streets and cities.

They sailed across several seas.

They searched fields and forests . . .

. . . mountains and deserts.

But they couldn't find the cunning tiger and the wild wolf.

When they were hungry,
they had to hunt for food.
So they couldn't eat
and eat and eat.

When they were thirsty, they had to look for water.
There was no time to sleep and sleep and sleep.
They were too busy trying to stay alive.

At last, they came to the jungle.
They looked high and low, but the cunning tiger
and the wild wolf were nowhere to be seen.

"Wherever can they be?"
said Flabby Cat.

"I bet they've gone to our house!" said Slobby
Dog. "I bet they're sitting on our sofa!"
"That's just the sort of thing a
cunning tiger and a wild wolf
would do!" said Flabby Cat.

So they went home to look for them.

Out of the jungle, back over the mountains.

Through deserts, forests and fields.

Over the sea, into the city and the street where they lived.

They ran indoors. "There they are!" shouted Slobby Dog,
pointing at the mirror. And right there, standing in front of the
sofa were none other than . . .

. . . the wild wolf and cunning tiger!

Or so they thought.

But the wolf was Slobby Dog all strong and slim from climbing and walking. And the tiger was Flabby Cat all sleek and trim from striding and stalking.

They gazed at their reflections and for the first time in a long time, they felt really comfortable with who they were.

All of which had nothing to do with the size of their sofa . . .

and everything
to do . . .

with **getting off it!**